Dear Parent:
Your child's love of reading starts here!

Every child learns to read in a different way and at his or her own speed. Some go back and forth between reading levels and read favorite books again and again. Others read through each level in order. You can help your young reader improve and become more confident by encouraging his or her own interests and abilities. From books your child reads with you to the first books he or she reads alone, there are I Can Read Books for every stage of reading:

SHARED READING
Basic language, word repetition, and whimsical illustrations, ideal for sharing with your emergent reader

BEGINNING READING
Short sentences, familiar words, and simple concepts for children eager to read on their own

READING WITH HELP
Engaging stories, longer sentences, and language play for developing readers

READING ALONE
Complex plots, challenging vocabulary, and high-interest topics for the independent reader

ADVANCED READING
Short paragraphs, chapters, and exciting themes for the perfect bridge to chapter books

I Can Read Books have introduced children to the joy of reading since 1957. Featuring award-winning authors and illustrators and a fabulous cast of beloved characters, I Can Read Books set the standard for beginning readers.

A lifetime of discovery begins with the magical words "I Can Read!"

Visit www.icanread.com for information
on enriching your child's reading experience.

I Can Read Book® is a trademark of HarperCollins Publishers.

Huff and Puff and the New Train
Copyright © 2012 by HarperCollins Publishers.
Library of Congress catalog card number: 2013947669
ISBN 978-0-06-230504-6 (trade bdg.) — ISBN 978-0-06-230503-9 (pbk. bdg.)

17 18 19 20   LSCC   10 9 8 7 6 5 4 3 2
❖
First Edition

Huff and Puff

and the New Train

by Tish Rabe
pictures by Gill Guile

HARPER
An Imprint of HarperCollinsPublishers

Chug-a, chug-a,
chug-a, chug-a,
choo-choo-choo!

Here comes Huff!

Here comes Puff, too!

Chug-a, chug-a,
chug-a, chug-a,
choo-choo-choo!

Here comes a train
that's fast and new.

The new train said,

"I am fast—let's have a race.

I know I will win first place."

"We will race that train,"
said Huff.

"We will do our best,"
said Puff.

"Ready, set, GO!"
the new train said.

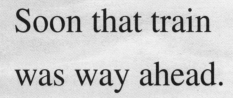

Soon that train
was way ahead.

13

The two trains raced
uphill and down,

in the country,
in the town.

The new train said,
"I am the best.

I'm way ahead.

I'll stop to rest."

"We're not fast," said Huff.

"We're slow.

But we won't stop.
We'll go, go, go!"

"Huff!" said Puff.

"We're going fast!"

Huff and Puff were first!

The new train was last.

"We did our best," said Puff.

"That's what we do!

I'm proud of us."

Huff said,

"Me, too."

Chug-a, chug-a,
chug-a, chug-a,
choo-choo-choo!